NEW EROTICA
for
FEMINISTS

NEW EROTICA
for
FEMINISTS

*satirical fantasies of love, lust,
and equal pay*

CAITLIN KUNKEL
BROOKE PRESTON
FIONA TAYLOR
CARRIE WITTMER

PLUME

PLUME

An imprint of Penguin Random House LLC
375 Hudson Street
New York, NY 10014

 Registered Trademark—Marca Registrada

Illustrations by Sarah Kempa

LIBRARY OF CONGRESS CATALOGING-IN-PUBLICATION DATA
has been applied for.

ISBN 9780525540403 (paperback)
ISBN 9780525540410 (ebook)

Printed in the United States of America
1   3   5   7   9   10   8   6   4   2

Book design by Joy O'Meara

For every hot and bothered feminist out there,
this book is for you.
We hope it makes you burn ... for equality.

🔥 🔥 🔥

CONTENTS

NEW SEX AND DATING EROTICA FOR FEMINISTS

*Love me Tinder. From sexy sweatpants to a new plan A
for obtaining Plan B, this chapter is all about love and sex in
the here and now.*

37

NEW LITERARY EROTICA FOR FEMINISTS

*Real-talk Jane Austen, self-aware Nick Carraway, and other
imaginings of literary lust.*

53

NEW POP CULTURE EROTICA FOR FEMINISTS

*All your favorites show up for a big ol' orgy of fictional,
empowering celebrity smut.*

67

NEW EROTICA FOR FEMINISTS
WHO ARE PARENTS

Parents have needs too, even if those needs are mostly just naps.

89

NEW EROTICA
for
FEMINISTS

FOREPLAY

Erotica is a written genre intended to arouse. Satire is a form of comedy designed to ignite. If erotica and satire made some questionable choices in the back of a Volkswagen van, their baby would be *New Erotica for Feminists*.

We would *love* for you to believe that when the four of us started riffing on funny feminist fantasies together one afternoon, we were thoughtfully deconstructing the patriarchy with erudite, highbrow wit from the get-go. In reality, we were goofing off in a group chat while editing The Belladonna (the comedy and satire site we cofounded, by women and nonbinary authors, for everyone), devising far-fetched and sensual schemes to convince the fine people of LaCroix Sparkling Water to deliver cases to us under the guise of a "corporate sponsorship." And hey, while we're speaking these desires into the universe, why not send, say, Tom Hardy to make that delivery?

This collective reverie turned into "New Erotica for Feminists," a short satirical piece made up of twelve original vignettes that ran on *McSweeney's Internet Tendency*. In the days following publication we watched, jaws agape, as our group cackle spread across the internet like wildfire. It quickly became clear that our erotic feminist daydreams had hit a deeper throbbing nerve, one that runs through every date, conversation, and breath of many a woman's life. It's the nerve that stands on end every time you see a "best of" list that includes exclusively men. It's the nerve that frays every time a date loudly talks over you to explain how important the Women's March was. It's the nerve that flares up when you're "mommy-tracked" at work, told to wear more or less makeup, given a side-eye for the food you order, or told to "smile more."

It was endless, bawdy fun to flip well-worn tropes of pornography and erotica. But the more we wrote, the *angrier* we got. Ah, yes, the angry feminist—the most erotic of characters! *Why* should these things—equal pay, decent maternity leave, construction workers who catcall about books rather than looks—have to remain so far from our grasp in 2018?

Can one book of smutty jokes bring down our problematic patriarchy? Sadly, no. (Unless you literally hurl it at a lurking creeper's nugget pouch in a parking garage; then, partially.) But as the serious and necessary global conversations sparked by the #MeToo and Time's Up movements continue, think of this book as your humorous release valve, providing a moment to laugh, think, and ignite the new batch of fire and energy we'll need to bring about our utopian future ruled by an immortal Ruth Bader Ginsburg.

Erotica invites readers to imagine themselves in different scenarios; our book is no different. We hope we've left just enough room in each vignette for you to slink in as the main character. In that vein, we've intentionally removed many identifiers to allow a diverse array of readers to superimpose themselves onto the page. While feminists of many ethnicities and orientations are celebrated and name-checked throughout, we strived to be responsible allies, rather than presuming to speak *on behalf of* another's experience or struggle. We've also included a resource chapter, inviting and emboldening us all to get more involved in relevant issues and step outside our normal spheres.

So get crazy, dear and sexy reader. Let's gather at the crossroads of personal passions and righteous anger. Grab your friend, spouse, or book club hookup, and let your wildest satirical fantasies flow.

Because there's nothing sexier than love, lust, and equal pay.

NEW EVERYDAY

EROTICA

for

FEMINISTS

The cop asks if I know why he pulled me over.

"Because my taillight is out?"

"Yes, ma'am. It's not a huge deal, but it could be a potential safety issue. I'm happy to escort you to a busy and well-lit garage a few blocks up run entirely by female mechanics. I won't give you a ticket if you can take care of it now."

"That's fair," I say, my eyes lingering over his clearly visible badge and identification.

"Congress is now fifty-fifty women," my partner whispers, pouring me a delicious glass of calorie-free wine. "And 'pro-life' no longer refers to abortion, but to a consistent position based on helping all people reach their fullest potential. Hey, would you like a foot massage? It's not a fetish, I just know how hard you work."

can see his massive bulge from all the way over here, despite the crowd. I feel a bead of sweat drip down my forehead, my blood boiling with every second that passes. I'm about to explode.

"Excuse me," I finally say to the man whose legs are open to an impressive 180-degree angle on the short park bench. "Can you move over a bit?"

"Wow," he says, horrified, snapping his legs shut with a THWAP. "What a reasonable request! I am so sorry I was dominating a shared space with my privileged body."

The doorbell rings. It's the plumber.

"I'm here for that very, very big job you needed done," he says. "Sorry I'm a few minutes late. I was liking all of Malala Yousafzai's tweets and lost track of time. I was a very bad boy and I'm sorry."

He toys with the zipper on his coveralls.

"You're clearly the man for the job," I say. "Lay some pipe for me NOW."

He lays my new copper pipes as we chat about the upcoming midterm elections.

I get catcalled on the street by a construction worker. He says that he can see I'm smart because I have enormous books. He tells me he's reading the latest Zadie Smith novel. I invite him to join my book club and spend all night fantasizing about his insightful commentary around nonlinear plot structure.

The pizza delivery car pulls up outside. It's right on time and so, so hot. The delivery guy hands it over with an appropriate smile and says, "Enjoy! I hope you're not sharing it with anyone if you don't want to. I believe everyone is in control of their own bodies and should never be shamed for what they decide to eat or not eat." He makes no effort to come inside because that would be weird and alarming. I smile and give him a reasonable tip for his normal behavior as I shut the door.

Time for *The Crown*.

He tied the thin white rope so tight that his fingers became red.

I couldn't believe this was *finally* happening. This unspoken tension between us had been the primary source of my frustration for years. I needed this to feel free. Hell, to feel anything.

He took out an even girthier rope. I felt my heartbeat rise as I stared at him, chest heaving. What more could he possibly tie up?

I held my breath as he pressed and bound, pressed and bound, tighter and tighter. It felt like it would never end. He took charge—God, I loved it when he used his hands. By the time he stood up and strode to the back door, his T-shirt clung to his sweaty torso. As the door clicked closed behind him, I slowly stood up, releasing a long sigh of total satisfaction.

I skipped around the empty kitchen with glee while he went downstairs to take out the bundles of recycling.

My hands flutter as I unbutton my blouse and slide my jeans down over my hips. I can't keep doing this, sneaking away in the middle of the workday to hastily get undressed, each session inevitably ending with more questions, more doubts, and no satisfaction.

Will this time finally be different? God, how long has it been since I felt truly seen? It's always about *his* timeline, his ego, his beliefs. The men are all the same at this point. "Negging" me until I feel lucky just to have a small sliver of their attention. I feel the knot in my stomach grow tighter as the door opens.

Except this isn't the man I expected. This is someone new, someone I've never seen before.

"I've reviewed all your laparoscopy results," my new female doctor says, "and I believe you when you say you've been in serious pain for a long time. I finally have a firm diagnosis for you: endometriosis. Let's work together to find you a quick and pain-free treatment plan."

This had escalated from flirtation to addiction so quickly. I needed the rush every day. Sometimes twice a day. And I knew exactly where to indulge my every intense craving.

My body shivered as I gathered the many sacraments of this lustful worship to me: oils, pillows, chocolates, and so, so many candles. Each time, I promised myself I just needed a little bit more, knowing I wouldn't—*couldn't*—stop there. I always lost myself so completely, so willingly.

I walked up to a woman in red, feeling her knowing gaze pierce me, *see* me.

"Wow, that sure is a lot of candles! Your total is $192.60," she said. "Thanks for shopping at Target!"

NEW WORKPLACE

EROTICA

for

FEMINISTS

He calls me into his office and closes the door . . . to promote me. He promotes me again and again. I am wild with ecstasy.

"I have to tell you something," I say, twisting my hands nervously. "And you probably won't want me after you know."

"I can't imagine a reason not to want you," he says, leaning forward.

I take a deep breath. "I'm pregnant. Sixteen weeks, to be exact."

"Congratulations! Our job offer still stands," he says without a pause. "We've been looking for months, and we're convinced you're the best director of finance out there."

"Well, then, I accept!" I seize a pen and sign the offer letter with a flourish.

An influential male journalist profiles me. He shadows me for weeks and weeks, bombarding me with intimate questions about my personal life and career. We share meals, long plane rides. I feel his eyes search mine, and I sense he's unearthed all my secrets. I feel known, understood, laid bare.

And, of course, he doesn't hit on me. And nowhere in his article about my raw talent, sparkling personality, and profound work ethic does he suggest a desire to have sex with me.

I step out of the steamy shower, rubbing a warm white towel over my athletic body. I'm alone, no one to see me in my nakedness. I take my time toweling off, slowly dabbing the moisture off my skin, everything exposed.

I hear footsteps behind me.

Whirling around, I frantically try to cover myself.

Then I relax and let my towel drop to the ground. It's just my teammate running into the locker room, still clad in her sweaty uniform with confetti stuck in her hair. I can hear the unrelenting roar of the crowd as the locker room door slowly closes behind her.

"Hurry up and get dressed," she says, giving me a high five. "They're about to do the trophy presentation, and every media outlet in the world is out there—we're going to get even *more* massive endorsements after this third-straight World Cup win!"

I smile. It's truly awesome to play women's soccer, the most popular and well-compensated sport in the entire world!

I walk into my office building, and a sharply dressed man walks in behind me. Feeling his eyes on me, I press the elevator button. It lights up.

The man doesn't press it again, just to make sure.

The firefighters arrive almost immediately and begin battling the blaze ignited when one of my dogs knocked over my pizza-scented candle.

Once safely on the front lawn, I cry out over the roar of the flames, "My dogs! My beloved dogs, Tina Spay and Amy Pawler, are still inside!"

"It's too dangerous—don't risk it!" yells my white male neighbor named Chad or Kyle who has probably never had to overcome adversity of any sort.

"Well, I don't know about you, but I'd rather die than let cute dogs named after my favorite comedians slash authors slash Golden Globe hosts perish," replies a shredded firefighter who looks like a genetic mash-up of Idris Elba and danger.

He rushes into the inferno. Agonizing seconds tick past—we're sure he's lost to the blaze. Until—oh, yes! In the heat, his sculpted outline reappears with Tina Spay and Amy

Pawler safely draped over his shoulders, snuffling him in doggie kisses of gratitude. His shirt has been artfully burned away by the flames to reveal a rippling, burnished torso, but—what's that tucked in his oh-so-very-slim fireman suspenders? He retrieves it and hands it to me.

"I couldn't help but notice you have some really rare first editions. You can replace your house, but you can't replace a signed 1970 copy of Judy Blume's *Are You There God? It's Me, Margaret.*"

Another long week spent servicing everyone but herself.

She was getting unbearably frustrated with this act—pretending she was *so* into them, that she was *so* eager to make their every desire come true. Why should she keep putting up with all the alpha-male bullshit when she knew she could get much better results in her bedroom, alone, by herself?

That is it, she decided. She was leaving the agency to start a business of her own.

"She's such a MILF," the venture capitalist says, staring longingly at the woman striding confidently out of the conference room.

"Seriously." Our CFO gives a low, drawn-out whistle of approval. "Now *that* is a Mom I'd Like to Fund. Her user-acquisition and retention rates are simply unparalleled."

"No," I say firmly. "That definitely won't fit in there."

The meeting immediately moves on to where in the report the new logo *will* fit.

And no one labels me a bitch for clearly expressing my professional opinion in my area of expertise.

"Who's your favorite comedian?" I ask the producer shyly after he compliments my set. *Please don't say Louis C.K., please don't say Louis C.K.,* I think to myself but also fully say out loud.

"Aparna Nancherla," he replies. "I can get you on a bill with her since I know her manager professionally. You could be a big star. But to be crystal clear, I'll do that regardless of any personal relationship between us. I just like to see talented, hardworking women succeed in comedy."

NEW SEX

and

DATING EROTICA

for

FEMINISTS

"Why don't we invite your friend over?" he suggests, testing the waters. "There's nothing I love more than watching two women in sweatpants engaging in hot political discourse. I fantasize about how you each . . . " He pauses, suddenly shy. " . . . always let each other finish without interrupting. I'll also make nachos!"

A stranger at a bar introduces himself, and the conversation is flowing.

He leans in close and murmurs throatily, "Would you like to get out of here and go to my place?"

"Oh, I'm gay," I reply.

"That's cool." He signals the bartender for another drink. "I've enjoyed talking to you. I won't try to convince you that you need to sleep with a man to know if you're really gay because only a huge jerk would do that. Anyway, did you also think *Dunkirk* was confusing?"

I slink into the bedroom, ready to surprise my partner with my brand-new fire-engine-red lingerie. Everything is on display, and I can't wait for them to take me in. Their eyes slide sloowwwllllyyy over my body, before stopping abruptly at my feet.

"Take everything off," they say, " . . . except those shoes. They make me crazy."

I peel it all off, leaving only my comfy, nine-year-old Birkenstocks.

I meet a scientist on Tinder. They go on and on about their biggest professional achievement: the serum that made Supreme Court justice Ruth Bader Ginsburg immortal. It drives me wild. I don my naughtiest jabot and grab my sex gavel.

"I'm sorry, but I'm just not up for that tonight," I say timidly, afraid he'll lash out at me. After all, I dressed up. Came out to a bar to meet him. Had a few drinks. Was I asking for it?

"No problem!" my date replies. "Actually, with like five seconds to think about it, I realize it's VERY inappropriate to ask the person I'm on a first date with to help me process my last breakup with someone they've never met. Man, emotional labor overload, am I right??"

With that behind us, we spend the next hour drinking Scotch and talking about the shared passion that brought us together: *The Legend of Zelda*.

"I really want to try butt stuff," he says breathily.

"You do?" I ask him with surprise.

We stare into each other's eyes for a long time. Finally, he breaks the silence.

"Actually," he says, "I really don't know. Society has conditioned me to believe that I should be constantly trying to up the ante, but to be honest, I really love what we've been doing and just want to do more of that."

"Cool, we can get Five Guys then."

"So, what do you do?" he asks as he stares into my eyes, not at my breasts spilling over the neckline of the dress I bought from Topshop but haven't felt sassy enough to wear until this Tinder date.

"I'm a nurse," I say, annoyed at the high volume of chatter in this make-your-own-gnocchi joint.

I can't hear his whispered response—something about being so hard? I'm sure it's something inane. Ugh, first dates! Suddenly, I regret every dollar of my meager paycheck I spent on this dress. He clearly doesn't deserve it.

"*Excuse* me?" I say, irked, showing it in my aggressive fold of the gnocchi dough.

"I said that must be so hard, being a nurse. You have the most important job in the world." He looks around. "Boo, it's too loud in here. Would it be okay if we left and went to this one-woman show about Margaret Thatcher I've been dying to see?"

We finish our third time that night in a tangle of sheets.

"Oh, no. I . . . I think the condom broke," he says. "Are you on birth control?"

"No," I say, embarrassed. "I was on the pill, but it made me so emotional and sad, and then I tried the patch, but it kept falling off. And I read way too many Yahoo! answers to get an IUD. I'm sorry!"

"I totally understand," he says. "If there was an equivalent birth control option for men, I would absolutely take it, no question. Women have been through enough."

His words make me delirious with desire all over again.

"What's your Venmo?" he asks, taking his phone out of his Strand tote. "Plan B is expensive, and I want to split the cost because of the pay gap."

"What's our safe word, if we get too wild in our equal-pay role play?"

"'Benedict Cumberbatch.'"

"Maybe it's time for some role play," my husband murmurs, trying to get me in the mood.

"Okay." I giggle.

"I'll be a big Hollywood producer, and you're a rising starlet."

"Hot," I say, nuzzling his neck. "Tell me more."

"I see your spectacular . . . talent and I treat you with respect." His hands are wandering. "I line up a female screenwriter, director, and cinematographer for your next film."

I moan as he continues.

"Your box office receipts are soooo big that studio heads are finally convinced that women-driven films are bankable. Not only that, Greta Gerwig wins her tenth Oscar."

"Yes!" I shout. "Cast me now!"

"No, I don't want to have sex right now," she says firmly.

"Okay!" he says cheerfully, taking himself and his boner out of the room.

And that is all the dialogue there is in my favorite porno, *A Hard No.*

JULIET CAPULET

APOTHECARY
YOUTH COUNSELOR
98 YEARS YOUNG

NEW LITERARY

EROTICA

for

FEMINISTS

His hand trailed across her breast, tracing a shape with his finger.

"I'm so glad that they didn't make you wear a scarlet letter after all," Arthur said. "I mean, you thought your husband was lost at sea. It was an honest mistake."

"It definitely was," Hester said, running her fingers through his surprisingly silky hair.

"I've also been thinking—your embroidery is so exquisite and the people here don't appreciate it. Want to move to New York and open a shop? I was thinking it might be nice to hire shunned 'fallen' women so they have livelihoods."

"YES," Hester cried, falling into his arms and starting the arduous process of removing nine petticoats.

Then they had really hot sex, by Puritan standards. So, just missionary with light kissing.

ROMEO

What lady is that which doth enrich the hand
Of yonder knight?

JULIET *sees him leering at her. Oh, crap, he's coming
over—she pretends to study a nearby ivy vine.*

JULIET

What sort of gentleman art thou?
All night thou starest as if I were a prize sow.

ROMEO

My name is Romeo, your humble servant.

He goes in for a kiss.

JULIET

(puts up hand in STOP signal)

Whoa, buddy, you can't just make a move like that without even asking my name. A little advice: Consent is sexy.

ROMEO

(seizes her hand)

My lips, two blushing pilgrims, ready stand
To smooth that rough touch with a tender kiss.

JULIET

(pulls hand away)

Gross! You haven't even asked my name yet!

ROMEO

Canst I fetch thou a drink?

JULIET

Um, no, Roman Polanski. I'm thirteen. What's next, asking me if I like hot tubs?

ROMEO

But we are star-crossed lovers . . .

JULIET

Mmmm, yeah, except no. We're not. You were drooling over fair Rosaline five minutes ago. This is a toxic relationship in the making, and I'm out of here.

JULIET *exits stage left*
and lives to be ninety-eight years old.

I've been here for hours—maybe even longer. All I know is that the sun is coming up. But every minute, every second has gone by faster than the last in anticipation of what's to come.

I've been entranced, my mind and my body completely outside reality. I know it's almost over, so I savor every moment, every chapter, every page, every line. I close the book in disbelief.

I just read a science fiction novel with zero violence against women to motivate the male protagonist!

was on my hands and knees, trickles of sweat running in rivulets between my breasts. I'd never wanted anything more.

And yet this wallpaper was just . . . so resistant. As I scraped, the tendrils and curls of the bilious yellow pattern seemed to adhere even more strongly to the wall. But that was ridiculous. Wasn't it?

I confided my worries about the wallpaper to my husband, John. He said that there must be a simple explanation, but regardless, my time would be better spent writing than stripping wallpaper. I sighed with relief. Other people might think it inappropriate for a new mother to work her way through her malaise by penning a novel, but my husband is a physician and understands the need for a vocation.

So we hired a handyperson to strip the paper and paint the walls a calming blue. I used the room as my writing studio and wrote a feminist novel for the ages.

"Why, hello, Dolores." The prospective tenant licks his lips as he eyes the young girl. "Does anyone ever call you Lolita?"

Just then, Charlotte, Dolores's mom, bustles back into the room.

"I'm sorry, I just performed a thorough screening—as I do with all potential tenants—and discovered you have a very troubled past, so I'm afraid I don't think you'd be an appropriate tenant."

As Humbert Humbert drives disappointedly away from their house, planning to set off on a road trip to find girls who remind him of Dolores, he conveniently hits a tree and is killed instantly.

Years later, Dolores goes to college and eventually becomes a professor of Russian literature—specializing in unreliable narrators.

stare into her eyes. My gaze lingers on her gorgeous face, her chest, down to her powerful, toned arms and her sun-kissed legs as she lies on the chaise in the dayroom. It's almost sunset.

For a moment, I think I love her.

But then the moment passes because I know that I am dull and selfish. She is tough, confident, and the most successful person I have ever known. All I do is party with my friend Jay, who has a pool.

I now realize that I, Nick Carraway, certainly do not deserve Jordan Baker, professional lady golfer. From now on, I will stop hitting on her, no matter how drunk we are at Jay Gatsby's house.

"My dear Mr. Bennet, it took only twenty-three years of marriage, but finally, all our goals have been achieved. Two of our daughters have married kind, accomplished, rich men! And Lydia is the wife of an officer, at least." Mrs. Bennet smoothed her hair with a satisfied gesture. "I just don't know what I'll do with all my spare time now that I'm not frantically matchmaking for our family's survival."

"I can think of something, Mrs. Bennet." Her husband slid his hands over her bodice and cupped her breasts.

"Ohhhh, Mr. Bennet!" She moaned. "Say, it just occurred to me that we have never been formally introduced. What *is* your first name? Mine is Bertha."

NEW POP CULTURE

EROTICA

for

FEMINISTS

I hear a box truck backing up in my driveway. Tom Hardy steps out, wearing a tight T-shirt that says WILD FEMINIST. He politely asks my permission to step inside to fill up my whole refrigerator with free LaCroix and play with my rescue dog every Tuesday forever. I consent clearly and enthusiastically.

The chains that bind me are cold. There's one around my neck, my wrist, each ankle. All of my chains bind me to him.

I am a captive of the Tatooine crime lord Jabba the Hutt, and the only good thing about this situation is that I'm wearing a very comfortable outfit: high-waisted pants (they really suck it all in), a shirt that covers my entire torso, and a sensible cardigan.

Now, on to my plan to save all of the captives on the *Khetanna*, including a Jedi (who is maybe my brother?!), the in-house band, and my love interest, Han Solo, by strangling Jabba the Hutt with the chains he bound me in.

I am his possession. All the fancy dresses and elaborate meals can never make me forget that my life exists now only for his unblinking gaze. I have everything—everything except my freedom.

My life as a bookish teenager in a poor provincial town feels worlds away now. It's almost hard to remember how desperately I longed to leave. Now I'd give anything to get away from this beast. Sure, he owns his own palace and throws great parties, but he also has a terrible temper and so much back hair.

He enters the West Wing. As usual, my master is not happy, and I await his punishment as I weep bitterly into my stupid enchanted mirror.

Except today, the beast says the words I have dreamed of.

"You can go," he says. "You . . . you have free will."

After saying good-bye to a candle, a clock, and a single-mother teapot who can talk, I hightail it back to my village to become an independent bookseller. The beast eventually goes to cognitive behavioral therapy and turns back into a handsome human.

We get back together, but, like, on my terms.

Ed Sheeran releases a new single called "I'm in Love with Your Body of Work," about Agatha Christie. It sells nine billion copies (more than there are people on the earth).

"You're a whore," he said, kissing her stomach softly. "I can't be seen with you."

"Umm . . . excuse me? You don't like it when people call you 'imp,' do you?"

"No," said Tyrion Lannister.

"Then I'd appreciate it if you called me a sex worker," she said. "You shouldn't diminish the services I provide, especially since you're willing to spend so much coin and travel all the way to Dorne for them."

I follow the rules.

I curl my hair and splurge on highlights that make me look even blonder, as requested. In fact, I dress up exactly the way he asks, knowing he's been dreaming of watching me do this for months: the right dress, the right heels, my sexiest Warbys— tonight, he wants me to role-play, to become *her*.

He finally calls me into the room. He gives me strict instructions, but I don't need them. I know exactly what he wants.

He's visibly impressed, but to be honest, I could do this in any outfit, any hair color, any day. In my fucking sleep. It's my job.

I'm very good at this, a natural. People say that I'm the best in the business, maybe the best this business has ever seen.

He gives me the part.

I am Meryl Streep, and you can see me in the second season of *Big Little Lies*.

During our daily FaceTime, I mentioned I was having a bad day.

An hour later, my doorbell rang. And there he was, flowers in hand, with just the tip of a firm baguette rising from his Whole Foods bag.

"I'm making you homemade spaghetti," said my friend and the internet's boyfriend Jeff Goldblum.

"Umm, Jeff . . . This is really sweet, but just so you know, I have a partner."

"I know! Of course I know that! This is for both of you amazing humans! We must embrace the ephemeral beauty of each day, of each, ah, ah, fleeting, ah, moment!

"Now, is it okay if I also clean your bathroom while quoting your favorite lines from *Jurassic Park* and *The Life Aquatic with Steve Zissou*?"

"Cap? Where do you think you're going?" Tony Stark barks across the Wakandan field as they fight Thanos, the supervillain threatening to destroy half the universe for his own gain.

"Um, yeah, sorry, team," Captain America says. "I get that this Thanos fight is important, but I read this really great book by an exciting writer named Roxane Gay on the Avengers' plane over here from New York. It really put things into perspective for me.

"I think the real battle that needs fighting right now is the Infinity War for gender equality."

She felt the vibration against her skin. God, it felt so good, so freeing, so . . . sensual.

She shook the long blond hair from her shoulders onto the floor, smiling at her reflection in the mirror.

Rapunzel was strictly a buzz cut babe from here on out.

"**Y**ou've been a very, very, very *bad* girl, Harley," he said. "In fact, on our next crime—and on all subsequent crimes—I think you should take the lead."

"Awwww, thanks! But honestly, I'd prefer it if you called me a bad *woman*," said Harley Quinn.

"Okay! I totally respect that," said the Joker. "You're the baddest *woman* for the job of murdering most of Gotham!"

"That means a lot. Now let's go destroy Batman—as equals."

"Tell me your wildest fantasy," he said, fluffing the pillow under his head.

"That people will stop asking why I never had kids," Helen Mirren answered immediately. "Also, to be the next Bond girl. Well, I guess it would be Bond *woman*. Actually, come to think of it, I'll just be the next Bond."

"So I hear that everyone likes to fantasize about at least one of the Chrises," he says.

I nod, blushing.

"Me too."

I raise my eyebrows. I knew he had wide-ranging tastes, but we've never gone into detail.

"Oh, really? Who's your favorite Chris, baby? Chris Pratt? Chris Pine? Chris Hemsworth?" I murmur.

He leans in to whisper his dirty secret.

"Chris Evert." Now he's the one blushing. "Nothing turns me on like a groundbreaking tennis legend."

$\bigwedge$ man sits at his desk, scrolling through an endless parade of twenty-one-year-olds on his monitor. His glasses keep falling down his face, a five-o'clock shadow starting to show. He's been at it for hours and has found no one who sparks his interest.

But then he comes across a young woman who finally intrigues him. She's a sorority girl (not the type he's usually drawn to), has great ratings (very important), and she has an inspiring, if sad, story (his personal favorite).

It's different from his usual fare: Her dreams of working in the fashion industry shifted after her boyfriend, Warner, suddenly dumped her at a restaurant when she thought he was going to propose. Brutal!

An unconventional track for a Harvard Law student, sure, but this young woman is curious, motivated, and unable to accept unfair circumstances—all the things he looks for. He wants to watch her arc unfold all the way to its exciting climax.

The dean accepts Elle Woods into Harvard Law School, Class of 2004, without wondering if she's hot or not.

"**I**'m so scared," she says to the young man she lost her virginity to hours ago. "I'm so c-c-cold."

"I know, I know," he says gently, but not condescendingly. "I'm here for you, Rose! Here's a giant door you can float on so you don't die of hypothermia."

"Let's share it, Jack! Based on my intimate knowledge of your body and my fairly advanced understanding of physics, I can tell that the cubic space available to us on this door would more than support our combined body weight when contrasted with the incredible buoyancy of salt water."

"Rose, I wish I had a good education like you," Jack says, climbing on.

They both live.

NEW EROTICA
for
FEMINISTS
WHO ARE PARENTS

I see the DM pop up on Slack. It's from *him*. My heart sinks—it's been two weeks since it happened, and this is the first I've heard from him. I have no idea what he's going to say, what he's going to *want* from me, now that I've crossed this barrier forever.

Skimming the message, my mouth drops open in shock.

"I know I'm the last person you want to hear from right now, but this can't wait. I saw your name pop up online, so I need to be clear: just delete Slack entirely and reinstall it when you're back," it reads. "You created a human being, NO WORK ON YOUR MATERNITY LEAVE!"

"PS: This won't affect your annual performance bonus—you're too valuable to the team!"

take a deep breath. I know I need to be bolder in reaching out for the things I desire. She's exactly the type of person I want to be with.

"Would you like . . ."

She raises her eyebrows at me. Overcome, I let the words out in a rush.

" . . . to set up a playdate between the kids this week?"

My favorite mom at the park smiles.

"I was about to ask you the same. I'm so relieved to find another parent I genuinely enjoy spending time with!"

"I've been thinking it might be time to try the thing we've always talked about. Why don't we call that woman we met . . . Jenna . . . and have her come over tonight? Let's have some fun!"

I hesitate. We've never done this before. It feels so dangerous and forbidden, but a part of me is dying to say yes.

"I don't know . . ." I protest halfheartedly, but he can see how excited I am, and I can tell he's so into the idea.

"Don't be nervous, let's just have a little fun. No judgment."

I giggle shyly and pick up the phone.

Soon, Jenna arrives and removes her coat. She's young and perky. I can already tell she's done this sort of thing before. I'm hit with a pang of nervous guilt and briefly consider calling the whole thing off, but we're past the point of no return. We've fantasized about it for years but always backed out at the last minute. Not this time. It's happening.

I slowly step toward her and whisper, "Thanks so much for coming over. We're *both* so excited you're here. Anyway, Jayden has just gone to sleep. We'll be at a 9 P.M. showing of the new Star Wars movie, the one that's just Laura Dern in space."

She happily and ably watches over our son for a fair wage while we enjoy the movie and a lovely meal at the Cheesecake Factory.

"God, you're amazing," she cooed. "You're sooo good.

"You've got that baby totally appropriately dressed for the weather, and I don't feel the need to interfere with your parenting or dictate whether you should work or stay at home," continued the total stranger on the street, smiling at my child and then continuing on her merry way.

"Tell that to me again," I whisper into her ear. "It made me soooo excited."

"You don't have to pack lunch today." She toys with a strand of my hair. "In fact, you won't have to ever again, Abby. Our kids have decided they're old enough to plan and pack their own lunches. Every. Single. Day."

"YES!" I scream. "YES, YES, YES!"

At first, it had seemed like a fun adventure, but now it was moving well beyond my comfort zone. The novelty had worn off, and it was starting to get uncomfortable. I was on the verge of breathing too heavily to continue, AND I was chafing.

Just as I was reaching my breaking point, a beautiful woman appeared in front of me.

"Need a hand?" she said, reaching down to grab the front of my double stroller and easing my way up the subway stairs. "It's so disgraceful that the elevators are always out of order at this station."

"**B**ut I want us to come together," he said.

She sighed. "We don't have to come together *every* time . . . even if your grandmother expects it."

"You're right," he said. "You should rest. You just gave birth to our third baby and an heir to the British throne. I'll take him out and show him to the crowd."

"Cool, thanks. I love you, Wills." Kate sank back onto her pillow, picked up the remote, and flipped to *The Great British Bake Off*.

Now on to more important matters than royalty, succession, and tradition . . . She'd finally understand how profiteroles were made!

"We're finally alone." I stand on my tiptoes and whisper into my husband's ear. "Race you!"

I take off, giggling, shedding my clothes as I hurry toward the bedroom. I can hear his footsteps close behind me.

I leap into the bed, nestling in the soft pillows. I slide a mask over my eyes.

He enfolds me in his arms. "Aha! Now I've got you."

"I'm so excited . . . to sleep." I turn on my white noise machine and turn off the baby monitor.

"God, I know!" he murmurs drowsily. "We'll have to take your parents to dinner. Taking on twin two-year-olds for a weekend? They deserve to be sainted."

We drift off into uninterrupted slumber for fourteen whole hours. It is orgasmic.

"It's . . . feeling . . . very . . . tight . . ." I manage to get out, panting and starting to sweat. Wasn't this supposed to be a pleasurable experience?

"Oh, then reach over the door, here's a magical flowy tunic that still somehow gives you a shape," the saleswoman says, handing me the new top. "You're only forty-three months post-partum after all!"

I open my blouse, my naked breasts peeking through for a fleeting moment.

I breastfeed my child in public. It is extremely uneventful and everyone is chill about it.

NEW HISTORICAL
EROTICA
for
FEMINISTS

ADAM AND EVE:
A RETELLING

The Lord God said, "It is not good for man to be alone. He will just lie prostrate, imbibe of the marijuana, and play *Call of Duty* all day. I shall make for him a partner."

So the Lord God caused the man to fall into a deep slumber by feeding him a large quantity of Burger King. While he slept the deepest of sleeps, the Lord God took out one of his ribs and closed up the place with flesh. With that rib, He fashioned a woman, and He brought her to the man.

The man said, "This is now bone of my bones and flesh of my flesh; she shall be called 'woman,' for she was taken out of man."

And she replied, "I can name myself, *thankyouverymuch*. I'm Eve."

Adam and Eve were both naked, and it was good. They felt no shame because they hadn't been subjected to a lifetime of lingerie advertising that programmed them to accept ridiculous societal beauty standards. They had a *lot* of hot garden sex.

Now the Lord God had made Adam and Eve a garden of many delights—an awesome river, very good trees, and totally free health insurance. He forbade them just one thing: the fruit from the tree in the middle of the garden.

Enter the serpent. The serpent was craftier than any of the other wild animals the Lord God had made, even more so than any of the Real Housewives. He slithered up to Eve and started stirring the pot with his serpenty ways.

"The Lord God knows that when you eat from the tree your eyes will be truly opened, and you will be like God, knowing both good and evil." When the woman heard that, she considered the source and quickly decided to do some follow-up research on her own rather than trust in a fucking talking snake.

After conducting rigorous scientific experiments that resulted in the publication of a well-received paper in *Nature*, Eve decided it simply wasn't worth the risk. She continued eating the free, locally sourced, organic pears and berries provided by the Lord God, and having guiltless naked sex with the lights on and painless childbirth as it pleased her.

Eventually, Adam was evicted for eating the apple when he had the munchies. Now it's quiet in the Garden of Eden, and Eve can work on writing her raw food cookbook in peace.

"Yes, yes. Almost there. Yes!" her partner screams.

The light flickers, reflecting the frantic excitement in the air. As the room gets darker, it gets warmer and wetter. The candles reflect the sweat off their glistening muscles as they approach the climax.

But she can't stop now. After all this time, she's done it. With the help of her brilliant partner, she's finally reached her life goal. All that they've worked for, for nearly a decade.

The historians finally have discovered the true meaning of Stonehenge: an advanced calendar built by ancient Druid priestesses to track their periods.

PARIS

Wondrous Helen, your beauty, bestowed upon you by the gracious goddess Athena, has enchanted me. I simply must have you. Come! Leave your husband, King Menelaus of Sparta, and sail to Troy with me, completely consequence-free!

HELEN

Hey, thanks but no thanks, P.

PARIS

I simply see no reason not to!

HELEN

Look, my life isn't perfect, but you'd have to be a real dummy not to see that my husband's brother, Agamemnon, is itching to have Sparta attack Troy, and me dipping out with you would be the impetus he needs to make that happen, politically. You with me so far, buddy?

PARIS

Ummmm . . .

HELEN

Plus, if you knew ANYTHING about me, you would know I've already BEEN abducted once before, by Theseus when I was younger. And guess what: It totally sucked! My husband won me in a contest, if you can believe that garbage. And all those guys who wanted me but lost to Menelaus swore to come to his aid if I were ever taken from him again. So you, my friend, would be in a whole Hades-load of trouble.

PARIS

Whoa, really?

HELEN

How do you not know this? It's like you haven't even read Herodotus. You *really* need to brush up on the geopolitical history of this volatile region, tiger.

PARIS

But you're so pretty!

HELEN

(*sigh*) I wish I'd been born a centaur.

"A little to the left," she directed, growing excited and quickening her pace as they grew ever closer. After a bumpy start, they were finally near the big finish.

"Are you sure?" asked her companion, panting with exertion.

"That doesn't seem right," said the second man, jostling for space.

"Do you trust that I know where it is, or don't you?" she snapped. "Should we just give up and stop right here?"

"Don't stop," both men pleaded in unison.

She resumed her steady pace, summoning her focus and thinking about the task at hand.

"I'm almost there . . . Just a littlllleeeee to the left . . . Yes, yes, yes, there it is!"

The Lemhi-Shoshone woman Sacajawea emerged from the thick bush, proudly leading Lewis and Clark to their first sight of the beautiful Columbia River in Oregon.

They'd reached the promised land, with her as their capable guide—proving that for every two men who "discover" something, there's a woman giving them directions.

THE "MY DAY" COLUMN
THAT NEVER
MADE IT TO PRINT

by Eleanor Roosevelt

Washington, Wednesday—I began the day as I do so many, taking the *New York Times* and a poached egg and toast in my bedroom. Missy brought Franklin breakfast in his study for two whole hours. It's so good of her to keep his spirits up.

I lunched with the Woman's Press Club and was happy to meet the president of Czechoslovakia in the garden. After a fine luncheon, the first afternoon musical took place. Mr. James Smithee sang three delightful groups of songs, and Miss Elizabeth Carrington gave us some very amusing recitations.

Unfortunately, we are suffering through a snowstorm. I was fully prepared to walk up to the riding stables for a turn with my favorite horse, Mr. Sour Pickles, but thinking the day too full of engagements, my soulmate, Lorena Hickok, and I instead retired to my quarters at Hyde Park for our own saddle work. We imbibed of one another deeply and in the most glorious nakedness, as if the spirit of Eros himself had touched us. Oh, her apricot bosoms! Oh, her amber waves of grain!

Back to earth again for fifteen minutes' talk with a most dynamic personality, Mr. George Swanson, who has taken on a most useful bundle of government homestead projects in North Carolina. Then five minutes' drive to the National Broadcasting Company building and back, then home to the drawing room to speak to some of the bright and helpful youth at the local YMCA. They presented me with a plaque. How lovely indeed.

And that, dear readers, is my day, as plain as yours, and

yet hopefully as steadfast in its commitments. Until tomorrow, I must retire to my private room that I do not share with dear Franklin for many reasons I have no time or inclination to explain here.

Until tomorrow, I'm off to Beavertown!

—*E.R.*

"What are your fantasies, Pierre?"

He took a deep breath, nervous to share his dreams with her. She smiled encouragingly. *I can trust her,* he thought to himself.

"It would be a beautiful thing, a thing I dare not hope, if we could spend our life near each other, hypnotized by our dreams: your patriotic dream, our humanitarian dream, and our scientific dream."*

"Well, darling, I meant more like 'Are you into dirty talk?' but that sounds amazing too," Marie Curie said breathlessly. "Let's do it."

And they did! Marie and Pierre went on to win a Nobel Prize in Physics together in 1903. Then Marie won a *second* Nobel Prize, for chemistry, in 1911—no man required.

Oh, and their daughter ALSO went on to win the Nobel Prize, because we all turn into our mothers eventually.

Actual quote from Pierre Curie, as he was trying to persuade Marie to marry him.

Reverend Samuel Parris has been staring at a dozen naked women for hours.

He studies every curve in each of their different bodies—some muscular, some pear-shaped, some fat—as the women dance, sing, and chant words he can't understand around a fire in the middle of the Salem, Massachusetts, woods. His hands tremble as, still staring intently, he reaches down into his pants . . .

. . . to get his notebook. In it he writes, in all caps and underlined, "<u>WOMEN OF ALL SIZES AND SHAPES ARE BEAUTIFUL IN THEIR OWN UNIQUE WAY</u>."

Parris watches for five more minutes (any longer would make him a perv, and he is a man of God). He goes back home to the cabin he built and never mentions what he witnessed to anyone, ever.

He and Tituba, who has not been driven mad by persecution, start a monthly body-positivity meet-up for teen girls.

14 WAYS

to

MAKE OUR

FANTASIES

a

REALITY

So . . . that was fun, huh? We hope you enjoyed that as much as we did! Now, as we lie here basking in the afterglow, let's get real for a sec.

We just used an entire book of comedy to point out some of the ways in which women are expected to live up to society's impossible and often conflicting standards. In other words, satirical feminist erotica is fun, but also more than a *teensy* bit enraging; after all, why are some of these simple fantasies still so far out of reach? We've all come so far together, but we still have so far to go.

If you're the kind of person who finds feminist satire compelling enough to have read all the way to this point in the book (truly, bless you), we're guessing you agree that it's important to contribute to creating a better, more equitable world for all (cue inspirational Kelly Clarkson song of choice). But between crucial everyday life stuff like work, parenting, or getting the dog down three flights of stairs before he pees, it's hard to carve out spare time to dismantle the patriarchy. We're all really busy people, and let's face it: Even simply reading the news can be emotionally exhausting these days.

Whatever your cause (and allotment of time and resources), you can spark progress. And even if you don't have a Malala-size platform of influence, we truly believe we can each move the needle in our own impactful way. Whether you're participating in a protest, standing up against someone making misogynistic or hateful comments to a stranger, or signing an online petition to advocate for equal pay while eating brie in bed (arguably the sexiest possible activism), the method and bandwidth is different for everyone. And, of course, intersectional feminism means equality for ALL, so it's important for those with platforms and privilege to actively participate in and learn from movements like Black Lives Matter and Families Belong Together.

Here are fourteen totally doable potential ways to jump in with us and feminists worldwide to help make our fantasies a reality. Remember, you don't have to do everything to make a difference (we need this freeing reminder); we all just need to find our something. But hey, if you're doing all fourteen, could we maybe hire you to be our life coach? Because, honestly, kudos.

READ: In the mood for some afternoon delight? Then it's time for a roll in the hay . . . with a good book. Reading is a simple, go-at-your-own-pace way to continue to educate ourselves on issues of gender, race, class, and equality. Slink sexily into the local library and/or (to spice things up even more) buy books from a diverse group of authors to learn more about intersectional feminism.

VOLUNTEER: Show up and put out . . . as a volunteer, that is. Offering our time, expertise, and perspective to pro-women organizations can help often limited resources stretch further. Ooh, nonprofits are *so* flexible! Volunteer with wild abandon.

SPEAK: Make noise to draw attention to good behavior and bad! If someone says something that strikes us as misogynistic or hateful, let's commit to use our words boldly by stepping in, reporting, whistle-blowing, and/or being an ally, even when it's hard or socially awkward or (gasp!) impolite. This isn't so much "dirty talk" as "real talk."

GIVE: Because giving can feel just as good as receiving. Recurring donations make a huge difference (even if it's modest—we know not everyone is loaded with ca$h money!).

If you do happen to be loaded, add zeros as appropriate and feel the pleasure of giving again and again and again.

LISTEN: An easy way to get some . . . perspective. Podcasts are a great way to widen our understanding of a variety of issues. In addition to taking in digital media, let's make an effort to listen to the experiences and opinions of people from different backgrounds, and stimulate ourselves aurally. Bonus: We can even do it in public.

HIRE: Our favorite position is a position to hire. Time to put on our blindfolds and hire fairly from the widest range of possible candidates! A few examples include blind-reading application materials, advocating for companies to conduct implicit-bias workshops, and working hand in hand with organizations that help train and place qualified women—especially women in marginalized communities—in a given field. Go ahead, switch it up and get adventurous.

CALL: Get more bang for every buck. Reach out and grab . . . the attention of our elected representatives on feminist issues, even if it doesn't have a direct impact on us personally. Because it truly takes a village to dismantle a patriarchy. We can also sign up to phone-bank or organize for feminist-friendly candidates for local and national elections. Let's murmur sweet political policy into voters' ears.

CLICK: Find and press that magic button over and over. There are a plethora of great websites that we can visit, read, and support that cover feminist issues daily in their own unique ways. The internet—turns out it's more than just porn!

VOTE: Wham bam, thank you, ma'am! Register to vote in your current area by going to www.usa.gov/voting, and vote. EVERY. SINGLE. TIME. It's the single most effective individual action you can take. Voting is the ultimate quickie—one and done, every time.

RUN: Let's get down and dirty! There are a variety of organizations designed to increase the number of women and minority candidates running for office. Let's whet our appetites with those and then get hot and heavy from there.

ORGANIZE: Talk about hooking up... If we don't see the thing we want, we can be bold and make it ourselves! It can be as small as a feminist book club or as big as an organized protest. Put in the work to make a thing, and the like-minded people will come . . . hard (hehe).

PARENT: Let's teach our kids about the birds, the bees, and oh, yeah, fourth-wave feminism. Parents and other amazing grown-ups can help kids understand that feminism is about equality, we all have the right to freedom from unwanted touches and gazes, and consent is key through reading and modeling. And as we're teaching our kids about feminism, we should emphasize that some women and non-binary people face even more acute levels of oppression based on race, religion, sexuality, class, and other social prejudices.

SUPPORT: Ooh, yeah, tap that network. Crushing it at work or in the side hustle? That's great—let's work to help other women and nonbinary people crush it as well! Answer questions or mentor as time allows, and pass along opportunities to those who are working hard and can benefit from them. It's so *hot* to rise together.

CREATE: Ready to get busy? Dirty talk alert: Putting feminist art and voices into the world can be a subversive and political act. Put that passion out there (in whatever form feels best) for the world to see, sexy.

For a living list of these resources, including links and more information, please visit our website at www.neweroticafor feminists.com/resources.

ACKNOWLEDGMENTS

The four of us would like to start by thanking all the wonderful, talented, creative contributors to The Belladonna. You inspire us every day, and we are all rising together! A very special thank-you to our interns, Nicole Martinez, Laura Scott, Kate Schulman, and Maddy Gross, who did so much for us while we got the book deal and then wrote the entire book. Remember their names and be nice to them, for they are coming to take over the world.

A tremendous and thundering thank-you to Chris Monks, the editor of *McSweeney's Internet Tendency*. Your kind, helpful, and polite editorial style influenced our own in more ways than you can know. We are also indebted to you for publishing the original piece, "New Erotica for Feminists," and for all the ways you've supported and encouraged each of us individually as writers over the years.

Not to be weird about it, but maybe we can meet in person someday?!

Major thanks to everyone who read and shared and wrote hilarious things about the original piece, showing us (and publishers!) that there was an appetite for more sex gavels.

Thank you to the editors and publications who have published and encouraged us over the years: Liz Kozak at the Second City, *Bust* magazine, *The Writer* magazine, Daily Shouts at the *New Yorker*, *McSweeney's Internet Tendency*, *The Establishment*, Marty Dundics at *Weekly Humorist*, and Elissa Bassist at Funny Women on *The Rumpus*.

Thank you to Plume and Sceptre for seeing what we were doing and hopping on board in record time! We are so proud to be affiliated with both of you.

A tremendous and major thank-you to Juliet Brooke at Sceptre, who messaged us out of the blue with the single best email any of us had ever received. Your energy, enthusiasm, and vision convinced us we could do this! It's been a privilege to work with you, and we've been "fizzing" with excitement ever since that first day.

To Katie Zaborsky and Jill Schwartzman at Dutton/Plume—your professionalism and cold hard KNOWLEDGE won us over immediately. Sitting across from you was like getting hit by a wave of smart feminist publishing info. We value our collaboration with you on this tight timeline more than you can know.

Thank you to the Thurber House in Columbus, Ohio, where we spent the final weekend before the manuscript was due eating tacos, reading "inspiration" erotica, and generally encouraging each other to "add more porny stuff" to the book. It was also the first physical place where the four of us internet friends were ever all in person at the same time, so it holds a special place in our hearts.

Thank you to the fabulous Caspian Dennis at Abner Stein in the UK for hopping on board with a day's notice and fast and furiously working out our contract. (By the way, you have the best name ever.)

Even though we are literally writers, we lack the right words to explain what our literary agent, Susan Raihofer of the David Black Agency, did for us. She took calls on vacation, taught us what a book proposal was, gave us edits on what felt like thirty drafts in ten days, encouraged us every step of the way with very fun email check-ins, got us paid, kept us sane, and sent us the conference dial-in information every single time we lost it. If you're going to do a big and hard and scary thing really fast, get you a Susan!

Thank you to the wonderful comedian and writer Sarah Cooper (of *The Cooper Review*) for being willing to generously share information that helped us make big decisions quickly. You get it and you are great.

Thank you to the excellent writers and comedians we admire so much who were kind enough to give us blurbs for the proposal: Jena Friedman, Jen Spyra, Scott Dikkers, Alexandra Petri, Sara Benincasa, and Anna Fields.

Thank you to the modern feminist writers and satirists who have inspired us to join them, albeit in a very different way: Jessica Valenti, Roxane Gay, Lindy West, Chimamanda Ngozi Adichie, Julia Pierpont, Nell Scovell, Amy Poehler, Tina Fey, Leandra Medine Cohen, Ijeoma Oluo, Emily Nussbaum, Inkoo Kang, and our fellow Plume authors Anne Helen Petersen and Phoebe Robinson.

Caitlin: When you've wanted to write a book for as long as you've had memories, it's a real challenge to know who to thank! I absolutely have to start with my parents, Monica and Larry, who gave me as many books as I could handle and never tried to discourage me from getting not one but TWO writing degrees. My father is a font of optimistic thinking when it comes to what a career can be. My mother is the hardest-working person I've ever met, and I'm truly blessed to have been forged in her image.

My sisters, Emily and Grace, are the most beautiful, smart, inspiring siblings a gal could ask for. We once argued about mozzarella sticks for literally hours, and it only made us stronger. Unbelievably, you found partners in Alden and Dru who are somehow just as amazing as you are. Are you witches?

Thank you to the Second City for training me and allowing me to instruct there, one of the great honors of my career. I've met so many excellent students, friends, and colleagues through teaching, I can't name them all. But know that you inspire me, you challenge me, and you show me new ways of looking at comedy and life each time I talk to you. If there's a better feeling than having a student become a collaborator and then become a true friend, I've yet to feel it.

To my friends who taught me how to be a creative professional. To my many coworkers and internet buds who mentored and pushed me. To the people who appeared in my life like they had always been there and hopefully will never leave.

To my dog, Zander—thanks for coming into my life this past year and patiently listening to me dictate feminist erotica into my phone during our walks. You're my bro, Zan.

To my beloved husband, Mike (last name redacted by request). A physicist and a comedy writer walked into a bar, and . . . well, I guess the punch line is that my life and marriage with you is better than anything I could have ever imagined. You support me in all the big and little ways, and your wholehearted belief in the weird stuff I've been doing made me believe in it too. How did I get so lucky to get you?

And honestly, thanks to Stephen King. Over twenty years of reading your writing woke up my mind in all sorts of ways. We kind of work in the same genre, right? Seriously—call me.

Brooke: Thank you, family: To my incredible and wildly hilarious husband, Gabe—a true partner, encourager, and man worth daydreaming about—for your tireless encouragement and labor to help me carve out the space to do this. To our brilliant and funny daughter, Arden, who is the best story we've ever started and who delights us all with each new chapter she adds to the universe. To our Lab, Margot Tenenbaum Preston, a sweet doof.

To my incredible parents, Ken and Carol, who cheered me in every play, choir performance, and article, and always made me feel, even in my tiny Ohio hometown (shout-out to Belpre!), that I could do big things. To my sisters, Tammy and Kim, who always make me laugh, especially in quiet places when it's very frowned upon, and support me whole-heartedly always. To my wonderful in-laws (the Sandusky Prestons, the Avon Lake Prestons, and the Robinsons), who love me as their own and don't even try to cover up the fact that I write professional joke smut. To the Scraggs for being my lifelong second family: Dave and Carrie for not minding terribly when we set accidental creek fires, and Ben and Sarah (Scragg) Filipiak for co-setting those fires and nearly all other formative humorous moments.

To friends who have loved me at my best and worst, even through a weird visor phase in college. My multidecade BFFs I met at Ohio University (go Bobcats!) have supported and shaped my comedy dreams when they were just dreams and are *still* most of the funniest people I know: Tracy Ewing, Megan Jacobs, Lesley and Ryan Sittler, Tony Frabott, Teresa Fisher, Jessi Marsh, Randy and Sarah Surface, Brooke Ignet Hocker, Mae Klingler, Lea Delaveris, Michele Minehart, and far more than any reasonable publisher would allow space for.

Newer but still dear friends have grown from casual comedy or preschool drop-off pals to true friends and helped me/us navigate the comedy/book-writing process with only the legally required minimum of tears: Christian Tucci, Kimberly Harrington, Riane Konc, Elly Lonon, Emmy Potter, Christy Jackson, you're the wind beneath my Chromebook.

Thank you to the Second City and Curious Comedy Theater (especially Stacey Hallal) for taking me under your wing when I was green and desperate for comedy fellowship—you trained, showcased, and later employed me (a humbling honor) so I could pursue comedy professionally as a working mom. Thanks to my high school drama teacher JoAnn Bartimus for making me feel like I could be more than a biggish fish in a tiny pond, and to my high school Advanced Composition teacher, Mary Finley, for making me a better, cleaner writer and doing so with grace and humor. Thank you to Tina Fey, Amy Poehler, Mindy Kaling, Jeannie Gaffigan, my spirit animal Anne Lamott, and more for being unbelievably strong and funny boss-mom writers who inspire me: I apologize in advance for embarrassing myself if we meet. And thank you, dear and sexy book buyer, for making this dream come true.

Fiona: Much gratitude and love to my husband, Daniel Delehanty, who is constantly hyping me and my work to anyone who will listen. Thank you to my soul sister and daughter, Arden, who wants to be many things (and would be good at all of them). I look forward to reading your fantasy novels one day! (Of course, I can't forget our cat, Ozzy, who is definitely a Hufflepuff.) I love you all so much.

Thank you to my fifth-grade teacher, Ann Leary, who told me I'd be a famous author one day (I've got the author part now), and also to my senior-year English teacher, Ann Birr, who told me I was funny and talented. Thank you as well to my art teacher, Leon Bryant, who encouraged my weird nerdiness and laughed at my jokes. Much love to my dad, stepmom, and sister, Chas Taylor, who is a fabulous writer and should write her own book ASAP.

Thank you so much to the female and nonbinary comedy community, which is incredibly welcoming, uplifting, and supportive. I love the way everyone is so eager to help everyone else, and I appreciate the friendships I've made. Thanks to the male allies in the comedy community as well! We can do this if we work together.

Thank you to my critique group, the Rogues, who are not comedians (although they are funny), but are fabulous people and writers: Karen Bischer, Linda Blum, Joanne Donovan, Danielle Rumore Lundquist, and Nancy Lambert.

(Agents/editors: Check out their work ASAP!) Thank you to my friends from school and my work life, all of whom encouraged me to write, even when I was afraid. I can't name you all (but I will hype my friend Daniela Amini, who is finishing her amazing literary novel). Love you all!

Most of all, thank you to my mom, whom I miss every day. I know you would be SO thrilled to see this in print (even if it might not be your sense of humor)!

Carrie: To my parents, who never said, "Maybe don't do comedy, Carrie"; to my sisters, Mary Maggie, Jennie, and Ellie; to my boyfriend, Nolan, who watched me cry a lot during this process and brought me McDonald's to make me feel better; and to our dog and biological son, Rebo.

A special thanks to my writing professors from the Savannah College of Art and Design: James Lough, whose wit, wisdom, and love for Devo inspired me to be as cool as he is (I'm not); Jonathan Rabb, who looked me in the eye and told me I was meant to do this; and Beth Concepcion, who made me better at news writing and other important things like writing professional emails, which I am still really bad at.

To my friends, old and new, especially Matthew Garber, whose talent, ambition, and encouragement got me to start thinking bigger for myself. And to my friends who don't know we are friends yet (Taika Waititi, Rachel Bloom, Tina Fey, and Kumail Nanjiani).

And to the small but lovely entertainment team at *Business Insider*, especially my editor, Nathan McAlone, who never edits out my Jar Jar Binks jokes. I'd also like to thank the entertainment writing community, which makes me feel better every day about my obsession with Timothée Chalamet and the fact that I do not understand *Westworld*—hopefully all of them are reading this?

And finally, to the incredibly patient people who follow me on Twitter.